Dr. Seuss's
ABC

HarperCollins *Children's Books*

TM & © Dr. Seuss Enterprises, L.P.
All Rights Reserved

A CIP catalogue record for this title is available from the British Library. No part of this publication
may be reproduced, stored in a retrieval system or transmitted in any form or by any means, electronic,
mechanical, photocopying, recording or otherwise, without the prior permission of HarperCollins
Publishers Ltd, 77-85 Fulham Palace Road, Hammersmith, London W6 8JB.

3 5 7 9 10 8 6 4 2

978-0-00-748775-2

Dr. Seuss's ABC
© 1963, 1991 by Dr. Seuss Enterprises, L.P.
All Rights Reserved
Published by arrangement with Random House Inc., New York, USA
First published in the UK in 1964
This edition published in the UK in 2012 by HarperCollins Children's Books, a division
of HarperCollins Publishers Ltd, 77-85 Fulham Palace Road, London W6 8JB

www.harpercollins.co.uk

Printed and bound in China

BIG A

little   a

What begins with A?

Aunt Annie's alligator . . .

. . . . . A . . a . . A

BIG B

little   b

What begins with B?

Barber
baby
bubbles
and a
bumblebee.

BIG C

little c

What begins with C?

Camel on the ceiling
C . . . . c C

BIG D

little   d

David Donald Doo
dreamed
a dozen doughnuts
and
a duck-dog, too.

ABCDE..e..e

ear

egg

elephant

e

e

E

BIG **F**

little f

F . . f . . F

Four fluffy feathers
on a
Fiffer-feffer-feff.

ABCD
EFG

Goat
girl
googoo goggles
G . . . g . . . G

BIG H

little   h

Hungry horse.
Hay.

Hen in a hat.
Hooray !
Hooray !

BIG I

little   i

i.... i.... i

Icabod
is
itchy.

So am I.

BIG J

little   j

What begins with j?

Jerry Jordan's
jelly jar
and jam
begin that way.

BIG K

little k

Kitten. Kangaroo.

Kick a kettle.
Kite
and a
king's kerchoo.

BIG L
little   l

Little Lola Lopp.
Left leg.
Lazy lion
licks a lollipop.

BIG M

little m

Many mumbling mice
are making
midnight music
in the moonlight . . .

mighty nice

BIG N

little   n

What begins with those?

Nine new neckties
and a nightshirt
and a nose.

O is very useful.
You use it when you say:
"Oscar's only ostrich
oiled
an orange owl today."

ABCD
EFG
HIJK
LMNO...

...P

Painting pink pyjamas.
Policeman in a pail.

Peter Pepper's puppy.
And now
Papa's in the pail.

BIG Q
little   q

What begins with Q ?

The quick
Queen of Quincy
and her
quacking quacker-oo.

BIG R
little   r

Rosy Robin Ross.

Rosy's going riding
on her
red rhinoceros.

BIG S

little s

Silly Sammy Slick
sipped six sodas
and got
sick sick sick.

T . . . . . T

t . . . . t

What begins with T?

Ten tired turtles
on a tuttle-tuttle tree.

BIG U

little u

What begins with U?

Uncle Ubb's umbrella
and his
underwear, too.

BIG V

little   v

Vera Violet Vinn
 is
 very
 very
 very awful
 on her violin.

W . . . w . . . W

Willy Waterloo
washes Warren Wiggins
who is
washing Waldo Woo.

X is very useful
if your name is
Nixie Knox.
It also
comes in handy
spelling axe
and extra fox.

NIXIE KNOX

BIG Y
little y

A yawning yellow yak.
Young Yolanda Yorgenson
is yelling on his back.

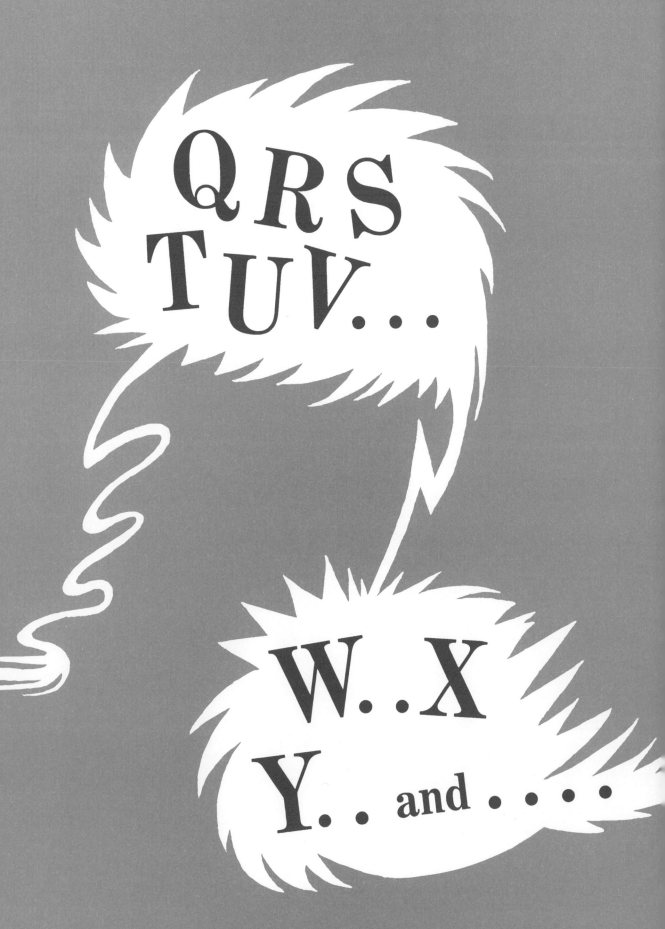
QRS TUV...

W..X Y.. and ....

BIG Z

little z

What begins with Z?

I do.
I am a
Zizzer-Zazzer-Zuzz
as you can
plainly see.